SCOOBY-DOO! PICTURE CLUE BOOK

PARADE PUZZLE

By Michelle H. Nagler
Illustrated by Duendes del Sur

Hello Reader — Level 1

ISBN 0-439-24235-5

12 11 10 9 8 7 6 5 4 3 2   1 2 3 4 5 6/0

Designed by Maria Stasavage

Printed in the U.S.A.

First Scholastic printing, April 2001

SCHOLASTIC INC.

New York Toronto London Auckland Sydney
Mexico City New Delhi Hong Kong

and his friends made a .

They taped on the .

They put on the .

And they blew up lots of .

"We're sure to win a ," said.

"Can we go now?" asked.

"I'm hungry."

Then locked the garage

with the .

Their would be safe.

But the  was not safe.

The was torn. The was spilled. The were on the floor.

"Jinkies!" said . "Who would wreck our ?"

"Maybe it's a !" said.

"Let's split up and look for clues," said. ", , and I will look outside. and , you search the garage."

 and did not want to look

for clues.

They wanted to eat and .

They heard a squeak behind the

.

"Zoinks!" said. "What if it

is the ?"

But it was only a .

 saw a scary shadow behind

the 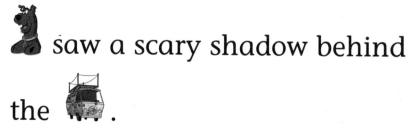.

But it was only cans.

"Like, what if the is still

here?" asked. "Let's look for

clues someplace else, ."

 nodded his head. "Rokay!"

 and ![shaggy] went to the

starting line of the parade.

The parade would start soon.

"Let's go check the ![ice cream] stand for

clues, ![scooby]," ![shaggy] said.

The man selling ![ice cream] did not see

anyone near the ![van] last night.

He had no clues.

But he did have lots of ![ice cream].

 and  saw  talking to the .

"I looked at your ," said a girl playing the . "I heard howling in the garage."

"I saw flashes of light," said a boy playing the .

"Like a ?"  asked.

"Yes! Like a ," the boy and girl said.

The 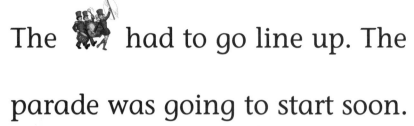 had to go line up. The parade was going to start soon. "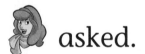, will you and go clean up the ?" asked .

shook his head no.

"Like, there's a !" said .

"Would you do it for a ?" asked.

"Rokay!" barked.

 and  went back to the

garage, but the  was locked.

"What do we do, ?"  asked.

 pointed his  at the .

"Good idea, ."

They climbed in the  and

cleaned up the spilled , the

torn , and the .

But then, they heard a noise!

"Maybe it's the !"  said.

But it was only , , and .

"How did you get in here?"

asked. "The was locked."

"We forgot to give you the ,"

 said.

 pointed his at the .

"We thought you were the ,"

 said.

 had an idea. "Wait!" she

said. "There is no !"

"There was a storm,"  said. "The wind and came in the open and ripped the and off the," said. "And it spilled the!" said. "Right!" said. "The wind made the howling noise. And the flashing light was." " and solved the puzzle," said.

and his friends made a new

 in time for the parade.

And they won first .

", we could not have done it

without you," said.

"Scooby-Dooby-Doo!"

 barked.

Did you spot all the picture clues in this Scooby-Doo mystery?

Each picture clue is on a flash card. Ask a grown-up to cut out the flash cards. Then try reading the words on the back of the cards. The pictures will be your clue.

Reading is fun with Scooby-Doo!